U0043759

Flower Shadows
40 Poems from The T'ang Dynasty

唐　詩　選　譯

Translated by
Adet Lin

林　如　斯　譯

Published by
Chung Hwa Book Company, Ltd.
Taipei, Taiwan
Republic of China

中華書局印行

FOREWORD

Miss Lin, daughter of Lin Yutang, spent almost 5 years translating these poems while she was also busy occupied with her other works in New York. These are favorite poems of her as well as of many other Chinese. She learned T'ang poetry from her father as a young girl, together with Chinese classics. And though she has spent the major part of her life abroad, she vividly remembers the countrysides and the seasons of China from childhood trips and her two years' stay at Kunming. It is this combination of personal experience plus hard work that has made these translations worthwhile.

Translation is an art, a work of love as well as a necessity for better understanding of Chinese culture. I find these translations refreshing and enduring. They are a good guide to appreciation of the Chinese original. Students and scholars would both find these poems useful. The moods and subtleties of T'ang poems are well conveyed, and the perfection of the original works in Chinse stands out even more illuminatingly through an understanding of both languages.

I am proud to be Miss Lin's superior at the National Palace Museum, where she has done many translations for the Quarterly, the Newsletter and other publications. I find her a sincere person, and write these few words in appreciation of her talent in rendering these short and famous poems of the T'ang dynasty into English.

Chiang Fu-tsung

December 1969

INTRODUCTION

By

Lin Yutang

The translation of Chinese poetry into English is a difficult art, not only because of the difference of the two languages, but especially to meet the requirement that, after the translation, the poetry still remains. There have been many efforts in this direction notably the worthy work of Arthur Waley. Some translations suffer from straining toward verbal accuracy, notably that of Florence Ayscough; others from the constraint of rhyme pattern. I do not think that rhyme need be always avoided, but rather that it has been the bane of many translations. Some translators have rested satisfied with the notion that so long as a verse form is in rhyme, it is poetry.

Good poetry often is the happy conjunction of sound and sense, of beauty of thought and expression. What makes it poetry is a certain elevation of spirit, which is given expression through deftly chosen, or happily natural words. The words which give form to the feeling are the clothing of the spirit. They may successfully and fitly match the spirit, or they may detract from it or spoil it. In this area of hard-to-define feelings, there are no prescribed rules. Either they fit, or do not fit. And this is so especially true of Chinese poetry. There are Chinese poems, both good and bad, those that come from a master pen, and those that reveal strenuous and even skillful choice of words in imitation of models. But all T'ang poetry usually in four or eight lines, concentrates on giving beautiful

1

form, often by indirection, to a momentary scene, or an exquisite, passing feeling. Often one has to say what one wants to say in twenty to twenty-eight words, or at best in forty to fifty-six words. Compression is the essence of such poetry writing. What is left is often a momentary picture, suggestion of what is not said. This is true especially of the short lyrics; in narrative poetry, one needs more lines, of course, and the poet usually writes in the "ancient" or pre-T'ang forms. Even in the short lyrics, one can prefer the "ancient" form, that is, free from the rigorous tonal patterns of the T'ang verse.

I think, in spite of the difficulties of the undertaking, the prime requisites are only two. First, the recognition of what makes it poetry in the original, and second, the ability to put it into English without losing that quintessence of poetry. The two are really one, the recognition of what is poetry and what is merely a commonplace conjunction of words. I am happy to recognize that the present translator has succeeded eminently in meeting this requirement.

Taipei, Taiwan
1970

2

CONTENTS

1

蘇 氏 別 業

·祖　　詠·

別業居幽處，到來生隱心。南山當戶牖，澧水映園林。

竹覆徑多雪，庭昏未夕陰。寥寥人境外，閒坐聽春禽。

1. THE RESORT HUT OF SU

Tsu Yung

This resort hut
　　set in a quiet place,
It becalms me
　　to come upon it.
The South Hill faces its
　　gate,
And the deep water reflects
　　its arbors.

Heavy laden are the
　　bamboos with snow,
The courtyard darkens
　　before dusk.
Lonely its seems beyond
　　human habitat,
So alone, I appreciate the
　　song of the birds.

山 房 春 事

·岑 參·

梁園日暮亂飛鴉，極目蕭條三兩枝。
庭樹不知人盡去，春來還發舊時花。

2. SPRING IN THE MOUNTAINS

Ts'en Ts'an

The crows are riotous at day's end
    in the garden of Liang;
Few scattered huts I see from here.

The courtyard tree remembers not the
    revellers have gone, and
With spring resumes the old-time flowering.

自遣

·李白·

對酒不覺暝，落花盈我衣。
醉起步溪月，鳥還人亦稀。

3. OF MYSELF

Li Po

Before my cups, I
  knew not dusk,
Fallen flowers scattered
  on my gown.

Rising tipsy, I trod the
  mooned brook,
Returning when birds had
  flown to nest, and
  the party thinned.

效崔國輔體三首之一

· 韓　偓 ·

澹月照中庭，海棠花自落；
獨立俯閒階，風動鞦韆索。

4. IN IMITATION OF THE STYLE OF TS'UI KUO FU-1

Han Wu

The moon has cast
　　its stamp on the center court;
The begonia, unattended,
　　drops of itself.

Alone, I watched from the idle steps
The ropes of the swing stirred
　　by night breeze.

4

效崔國輔體三首之二

·韓　偓·

雨後碧苔院，霜來紅葉樓；

閒階上斜日，鸚鵡伴人愁。

5. IN IMITATION OF THE STYLE
OF TS'UI KUO FU-2

Han Wu

After the rainfall, the green mossy yard;
Frost visits the red-leafed tower.

Idly, on the step, I stand in the slanting sun,
And the parrot, in boredom,
　　my company keeps.

效崔國輔體三首之三

· 韓　偓 ·

羅幕生春寒，繡窗愁未眠；

南湖夜來雨，應濕采蓮船。

6. IN IMITATION OF THE STYLE OF TS'UI KUO FU-3

Han Wu

That April chill
　　has invaded the nettings of gauze;
Fretfulness by the window pane...

Sleepless, I ponder: at the south lake
　　the rains must drench
　　the lotus-pickers' boats.

自 君 之 出 矣

·張 九 齡·

自君之出矣，不復理殘機。
思君如滿月，夜夜減清輝。

7. YOU HAVE GONE AWAY NOW

Chang Chiu Ling

You have gone away now
And I no longer tend the loom.

Thinking of you is as the full moon
that wanes night after night.

攜妓納涼晚際遇雨

·杜　甫·

落日放船好，輕風生浪遲。竹深留客處，荷淨納涼時。
公子調冰水，佳人雪藕絲；片雲頭上黑，應是雨催詩。

8. WITH THE LADIES OF PLEASURE
ON A SUMMER TRIP-1

Tu Fu

The sun sets—
　　　　a sailing time, when
Lately the breeze roused the wavelets.
In the bamboos, a nook for
　　　　entertainment,
Where the lotus clean awaits—
　　　　a cooling time.
The young dukes stir the ices, and
The fair maidens cut the caltrop sweet.
Thick clouds gather darkly overhead,
The rains fall, to poetry's hurry.

8

其　　二

·杜　甫·

雨來沾席上，風急打船頭。越女紅裙濕，燕姬翠黛愁。
纜侵堤柳繫，慢卷浪花浮。歸路翻蕭颯，陂塘五月秋。

9. WITH THE LADIES OF PLEASURE ON A SUMMER TRIP-2

Tu Fu

The mild storm had pelted the banquet mat,
The wind tilting the bow, rain drenching
The red skirts of maids of Yüeh,
Knitting the lovely brows
　　　of the belles of Yen.
Hastening, we stopped a while
By the willow bank, as wavelets shook
The bamboo screens and silk canopy.
On returning, the grey had lifted,
And a May day autumn greeted the wharf.

上 高 侍 郎

·高 蟾·

天上碧桃和露種，日邊紅杏倚雲栽。

芙蓉生在秋江上，不向東風怨未開。

10. FOR COUNCILOR KAO

Kao Tsien

The golden peach is nourished
　　with dew in the sky;
By the sun's glory, grows the cinnamon
　　on cloud puffs.
The eotus, floating on the autumn river,
Would not bloom save for the blessing
　　of the east wind.

Note – The imagery is artificial though original, and the poem
expresses gratitude for the patronage of Councilor Kao.

春　　詞

·劉 禹 錫·

新粧宜面下朱樓，深鎖春光一院愁。

行到中庭數花朵，蜻蜓飛入玉搔頭。

11. A NOTATION TO SPRING

Liu Yu Hsi

Freshly painted, the pretty one
　　descends from the vermilion tower,
To find spring light locked in a courtyard of grief.
　　She pauses before the few potted flowers, and
The dragonfly seeks and rests on her jade hairpin.

過　酒　家

·王　績·

此日長昏飲，非關養性靈。

眼看人盡醉，何忍獨爲醒？

12. PASSING THE WINESHOP

Wang Chi

The day is spent in long drinking—
'Tis not for health or good of soul;
I see all around me are drunkards,
For what reason should I remain sober?

破山寺院後禪院

·常　　建·

清晨入故寺，初日照高林。曲徑通幽處，禪房花木深。

山光悅鳥性，潭影空人心。萬籟此俱寂，惟聞鐘磬音。

13. THE ROOMS OF ZEN BEHIND THE ANCIENT TEMPLE

Tsang Chien

In the coolness I visit
　　the aged temple,
The early sun shines in the
　　tall forest.
The path winds through the
　　quieter places,
And the Rooms of Zen stand
　　deep in flowers and shrubbery.

The light of the mountain
　　pleases the birds,
The pond reflects the pure hearts
　　of the devout.
All interposition ceases
　　here;
And we hear only the sacred gong.

贈徐中書望終南山歌

· 王　　維 ·

晚下兮紫微，悵塵事兮多違。

駐馬兮雙樹，望青山兮不歸。

14. FOR MINISTER HSU LOOKING OUT ON CHUNG NAN SHAN

Wang Wei

Night descends on the purple nettle.
Discouraged that life is so full of obstacles,
Tied my horse by the pair of trees,
A spectator hence of blue hills without regret.

送　別

·王　維·

下馬飲君酒，問君何所之？

君言不得意，歸臥南山陲。

但去莫復問，白雲無盡時。

15. FAREWELL

Wang Wei

"Dismount, and have a tankard.
　　Where are you bound?" I asked.
You replied, "I cannot fill my ambition,
And shall go to the South Peak to sleep;
　　Pray ask me not again,
　　Somewhere the white clouds are endless."

鳥　　鳴　　澗

·王　　維·

人間桂花落，夜靜春山空；

月出驚山鳥，時鳴春澗中。

16. MOUNTAIN BIRDS

Wang Wei

In this corner,
The cassia from the tree idly drops.
The night is calm in the vernal
　　　　vale--hollow.
The rising moon startles
　　　　the mountain singers,
And to the vernal stream they fly,
　　　　to chant once more.

春　　暮

· 曹　豳 ·

門外無人問落花，綠陰冉冉遍天涯；

林鶯啼到無聲處，靑草池塘獨聽蛙。

17. LATE MAY

Tsao Pin

Outside the gate,
No more inquirers of blown flowers. . .
The group of green shadows undulate
　　even to horizon's end.
The forest canaries have sung their last.
One listens to the lone frog croaking
On the weedy pond.

春　　眠

· 孟 浩 然 ·

春眠不覺曉，處處聞啼鳥；

夜來風雨聲，花落知多少？

18. WAKING IN SPRING

Meng Hao Jan

To birdcalls everywhere loud,
I woke lazily from spring slumber—
Remembering the night's storm.
Ah, how many petals flew down to the ground?

尋 隱 者 不 遇

· 賈　　島 ·

松下問童子，言師採藥去；
只在此山中，雲深不知處。

19. VISIT TO THE HERMIT

Chia Tao

Under the pines, I queried
　　the lad,
"Where has your master gone?"
　　"Somewhere in the mountains
　　　　seeking herbs.
In the deep clouds,
　　I know not where."

曲 江 對 酒

·杜　甫·

一片花飛減卻春，風飄萬點正愁人。
且看欲盡花經眼，莫厭傷多酒入脣。
江上小堂巢翡翠，苑邊高塚臥麒麟，
細推物理須行樂，何用浮名絆此身？

20. ON CH'Ü RIVER

Tu Fu

A storm of petals
Has covered spring.
The wind, blowing a thousand dots,
　　saddens me.
Should I dizzily pursue to sight's end?
Better wine to the lips!
The little hall by the river now keeps
　　the kingfishers.
By the marshes on the high grave,
　　lies the unicorn.
To follow this logic my
　　pleasure I shall seek;
To what end, let empty Fame
　　bind this frame?

宿 建 德 江

·孟 浩 然·

移舟泊煙渚，日暮客愁新。
野曠天低樹，江清月近人。

21. BY THE CHIEN-TEH RIVER

Meng Hao Jan

The sailing craft is moored by the misty shore;
At sunset the guest encounters loneliness anew.
The sky over the wild fields is close to the trees,
And the moon above the waters comes near at hand.

漫　興

·杜　甫·

腸斷春江欲盡頭，杖藜徐步立芳洲。
顛狂柳絮隨風舞，輕薄桃花逐水流。

22.　CASUAL PLEASURE

Tu Fu

Winding-like as an intestine,
the spring river breaks
at the horizon.
Leaning on my cane, leisurely
I saunter to the verdant meadows.
The idiotic willow-buds freely
dance with the breeze;
The frivolous peach-blossoms
float by on the current.

山 中 問 答

· 李　　白 ·

問余何事棲碧山？笑而不答心自閒。
桃花流水杳然去，別有天地非人間。

23. DIALOGUE IN THE MOUNTAINS

Li Po

Ask me why I rest in the Emerald hill,—
A smile, wordless, and a leisure content.
The peach blooms, the running brook, go their way,
'Tis in another country that I dwell.

社　日

·張　演·

鵝湖山下稻粱肥，豚柵鷄栖對掩扉。
桑拓影斜春社散，家家扶得醉人歸。

24. COUNTRY FAIR

Chang Yen

Below the hill
By Goose Lake,
The rice grows fat.
The pig sty, and the
Chicken coop,
Are locked inside the gate.
Under the mulberry trees,
In the late afternoon,
The country fair disbands,
Each family takes his own
Drunkard home.

感　　遇

· 張 九 齡 ·

蘭葉春葳蕤，桂華秋皎潔。欣欣此生意，自爾爲佳節。
誰知林棲者，聞風坐相悅。草木有本心，何求美人折。

25. CASUAL THOUGHTS

Chang Chiu Ling

The orchid prospers in the springtime,
And the cassia in autumn attains lucent maturity.
I am glad of these living things,
I find it a happy time.
Who knows he who lives in the forest
Is joyous to hear the wind?
The grass and plants have their own;
They need not be cut by a maiden.

蜀 道 後 期

· 張　說 ·

客心爭日月，來往預期程。

秋風不相待，先至洛陽城！

26. DELAYED ON THE SHU PATH

Chang Yueh

The traveler's anxiety
Races with days and dusk;
So to keep his appointment, he is bent
On his destination.

But the autumn wind tarries not;
In advance,
It reaches the city of Lo-Yang.

秋　日

· 耿　湋 ·

返照入閭巷，憂來誰共語。
古道少人行，秋風動禾黍。

27.　AUTUMN DAY

Ken Wei

The umbrage has entered the lane.
Ennui, no one to converse with.
Few passers-by on the old road;
The autumn wind brushes the corn and wheat.

偶　　成

· 程　明　道 ·

雲淡風輕近午天，望花隨柳過前川。

旁人不識余心樂，將謂偷閒學少年。

28. COMPOSED AT RANDOM

Chen Ming Tao

The pale clouds, the gentle wind, at this
　　noon hour,—
Flower-watching, willow-threading, I go before
　　the stream.
Bystanders guess not at my heart's happiness,
Would say in idleness I seek to imitate the young.

蘇　臺　覽　古

·李　白·

舊苑荒臺楊柳新，菱歌清唱不勝春。

只今惟有西江月，曾照吳王宮裏人。

29. ON THE SOOCHOW PARAPET

Li Po

By the faded weeds, the tumbled
    parapet, new green the willows;
The water-caltrop pickers gaily sing
    a song of spring.
Here, too, lights the moon of West River.
That once illumed the decorous
    creatures of the Palace of Wu.

泊　秦　淮

·杜　牧·

煙籠寒水月籠沙，夜泊秦淮近酒家。
商女不知亡國恨，隔江猶唱後庭花。

30. BY CHIN HUAI RIVER

Tu Mu

Mist sieves the cold water,
Moonflow sieves the sands.
Moored by the river Chin Huai
Near the tavern at night.
The town-girl knows not
　　　surrender's disgrace,
Sings yet *Backyard Flower*
　　　over the night.

絕　　句

·杜　　甫·

兩箇黃鸝鳴翠柳，一行白鷺上青天。

窗含西嶺千秋雪，門泊東吳萬里船。

31.　FOUR LINES

Tu Fu

Two yellow orioles sing in the
　　sea-green willows,
A line of white egrets
　　climb up the blue sky.
The window confines the West Peak
　　with ancient snow;
By the gate, harbor the East Wu ships
that have sailed a thousand *li*.

草

·白居易·

離離原上草，一歲一枯榮。野火燒不盡，春風吹又生。
遠芳侵古道，晴翠接荒城。又送王孫去，萋萋滿別情。

32. ON THE PRAIRIE

Po Chu I

Desolate, the waving grass on the high prairie,
Mindless of yearly blight.
Wild fires cannot extinguish these weeds
        that revive every spring.
Now its soft fragrance invades the ancient route,
And the green bounty surrounds the tumbled citadel.
Once more farewell to the Dukes,
        Disconsolate, the waving grass.

Note – Emissaries from the Court made a yearly inspection trip
    to the prairies in the spring.

送　友　人

·李　　白·

靑山橫北郭，白水遶東城。此地一爲別，孤蓬萬里征。
浮雲遊子意，落日故人情。揮手自知去，蕭蕭班馬鳴。

33. FAREWELL TO A FRIEND

Li Po

Horizontal lies the azure hills across the North,
And the gleaming river goes 'round the
　　eastern town.
The long sail prepares for a journey of a
　　thousand *li*.
As drifting clouds, light and gay the whim
Of the wandering son, and
Wistful as sunset, the sentiments of the elders.
So farewell, and solitary departure.
See, how the bells jangle on the speckled horse.

送 友 人 入 蜀

· 李　白 ·

見說蠶叢路，崎嶇不易行，山從人面起，雲傍馬頭生。

芳樹籠秦棧，春流遶蜀城，升沉應已定，不必問君平。

34. FAREWELL TO A FRIEND GOING TO SHU

Li Po

I hear say like a silkworm winds the nettled path,
　　perilous for the traveler;
Strange cliffs rise before one's image,
And the curling clouds rest on the horse's mane.
Fragrant brambles crowd these shaky stairs of Tsin,
And the rough torrents circle the towns of Shu.
Alas, one's fate has long been sealed.
To the astrologer, Chün Ping, pay no heed!

芙蓉樓送辛漸

·王 昌 齡·

寒雨連江夜入吳，平明送客楚山孤。
洛陽親友如相問，一片冰心在玉壺。

35. FAREWELL AT PEONY TOWER TO HSIN TSIEN

Wang Tsang Ling

A cold troubled night, the night I came into Wu.
Now at dawn, I bid farewell to the departing guest,
The solitude of Mount Tsu remains.
If friends and relations in Lo-Yang ask after me,
Say, "Tis as ice in a jade pot, this heart of old."

Note – The author wrote in exile. The last line is very well-
known.

靜　夜　思

·李　白·

牀前明月光，疑是地上霜；
舉頭望明月，低頭思故鄉。

36. MOONLIGHT NIGHT

Li Po

Before the couch moonlight came.
I had thought it frost on the ground.
Looking up, I gazed on the moon,
And bowed my head with thoughts of home.

玉　　階　　怨

·李　　白·

玉階生白露，夜久侵羅襪。
却下水晶簾，玲瓏望秋月。

37. YU CHIEH YUEN

Li Po

The clean dew covers the jade steps,
The damp night seeps through my socks.
I should drop the crystal gauze screen,
But wait yet on the autumn
　　　　moon charming.

長信秋詞三首之一

· 王 昌 齡 ·

金井梧桐秋葉黃，珠簾不捲夜來霜。
熏籠玉枕無顏色，臥聽南宮清漏長。

38. LETTERS OF AUTUMN–1

Wang Tsang Ling

Scattered the golden coin leaves,
    autumn old on the ground;
The hanging beaded curtain
    frost-coated in the dark.
The perfumed pillow wane,
She lay listening
To the hours strike from
    the Southern Palace wing.

江　雪

·柳　宗　元·

千山鳥飛絕，萬徑人踪滅。
孤舟蓑笠翁，獨釣寒江雪。

39. SNOW ON THE RIVER

Liu Chung Yuan

A thousand hills,
　　all the birds have gone;
Ten thousand pathways,
　　all human footsteps
　　　　vanished.
The hooded fisherman
　　on the lone skiff,
Baits the snow on the
　　chilly river.

題 義 公 禪 房

·孟 浩 然·

義公習禪寂，結宇依空林。戶外一峯秀，階前衆壑深。
夕陽連雨足，空翠落庭陰。看取蓮花淨，方知不染心。

40. FOR THE HUT OF MASTER YI

Meng Hao Jan

Master Yi practices Zen
    in the quietude,
Chooses his hut by the empty arbors.
Outside his door, a rise
    of grace,
Before the steps, chasms
    deep.
The sunset follows on the
    feet of rain,
The hollow green falls on the
    terrace shady.
When he sees the lotus clean,
He knows his heart cannot
    be tainted.

ADET JUSU LIN was born in Kulansu, Amoy, Fukien in south China. She grew up in Shanghai and later went to the United States, studying at the Dalton School and Columbia University and continuing her study of Chinese classics at home.

In 1944, she went to Kunming as English secretary for the Chinese Army Medical Service and worked with Dr. Robert K. S. Lim there and in Chungking, until the end of the war.

Having studied poetry under Prof. Mark Van Doren and others, poetry has remained her main interest, though she has published a book of Chinese folktales for children and a novel under the pen name TAN YUN.

中華語文叢書

唐詩選譯（中英對照）
Flower Shadows 40 Poems from the T'ang Dyasty

作　　者／林如斯　英譯
主　　編／劉郁君
美術編輯／鍾　玟

出 版 者／中華書局
發 行 人／張敏君
副總經理／陳又齊
行銷經理／王新君
地　　址／11494 臺北市內湖區舊宗路二段181巷8號5樓
客服專線／02-8797-8396　　傳　真／02-8797-8909
網　　址／www.chunghwabook.com.tw
匯款帳號／華南商業銀行　西湖分行
　　　　　179-10-002693-1　中華書局股份有限公司

法律顧問／安侯法律事務所
製版印刷／維中科技有限公司　海瑞印刷品有限公司
出版日期／2018年5月再版
版本備註／據1970年6月初版復刻重製
定　　價／NTD 200

國家圖書館出版品預行編目（CIP）資料

唐詩選譯 ／ 林如斯英譯. — 再版. — 臺北市 :
　中華書局，2018.05
　　面 ；　　公分. —（中華史地叢書）
　中英對照

　ISBN 978-957-8595-33-0（平裝）

831.4　　　　　　　　　　　　　107004934